THE SUNRISE IS MISSING

SHAIK YASEEN AHMAD

Acknowledgements

For this book, there are contributions from many people, both directly and indirectly, who have inspired me, taught me, and supported me.

First and foremost, I would like to thank Shaik Hajna for her support in editing the book, providing great insights and advice to complete my first book, and making this book possible. I am eternally grateful.

I would like to thank my awesome sister, Shaik Rehana Samreen, for reading multiple drafts, providing feedback, and offering insightful ideas throughout, which have helped this book flourish.

A very special thanks to Aparnaa M for assisting me in the publishing process of the book and for always being a supportive, encouraging, and inspiring friend. You are an awesome friend.

I would like to thank R.L. Stine, the author of Goosebumps and one of the greatest children's book authors, for inspiring me and instilling in me the habit of reading books. You are the major inspiration and guide for this book.

I have endless gratitude to my parents, Shaik Mahaboobi and Abdul Hafiz Anamalamuri, for providing me with the resources to grow, learn, and create. I am always be grateful

I would also like to thank my college professors, Dr. Sankari M and Dr. V. Vijaya Bhaskar, for their guidance and for being extraordinary mentors in my life. I am eternally grateful for their teachings.

I would also like to express my gratitude to Sareena Ismath M and Chegoni Anusha for being the most supportive and inspiring friends.

Of course, I am eternally grateful to my extremely talented college club mates and my first teammates: Tummala Anupama , Sareena Ismath M, Hibha Kaleem, Rithika Raja, Sakthi Vinayak, Y. Varshita, Rakshitha K, Indhuja V, and Aparnaa M, for being a great team and an integral part of my growth. This team will always be special to me.

Special thanks to Anil Pallala, the CEO of Silly Monks Entertainment, and to Anil Putta and Prasad Bhimanadham, the team heads of Silly Monks, who continuously encourage me to become more creative and provide excellent guidance for my personal development.

I must also thank all the kind-hearted and extraordinary people with whom I have worked: Sk Shareef Pasha, Yeruva Raviteja, Batha Mounica Sai, Rahul Bhagi, Bhargav, Nagendra Ithireddy, Saiteja Sake, Srinivas, G Satyanarayana, Varsha, Aditya Kattu, Vishnu and Ramya Surenene, for their encouragement and teachings. They have imparted valuable skills useful for the book and for life. They are always ready to teach and share what they know. I love learning and working with you all!

Thanks to all my friends—Yashodhar Regatte, Yaswanth R, Y Hemanth Kumar aju, Seethalathevi, Katam Abhishek, Dhinakaran, Madhumita, Shivaranjani, Yeswanth Sai Abhilash, Gali Tharun Deepak, Karthik Varanasi, Gaikoti Dinesh, Heena Praveen, Mukesh Chitturi, Venkatalakshmi, LG Rushika, Preethi, Vasanth R, Shyam, Dinesh Vudatala, Rishitha Reddy Munnelli, Princy Adriel, Sravya Bharathi, Ashika, Nalin Prabhath, Vundemodugula Sowmya, R Joshma, Thilothama Drashti, Sai Mounik, and Venkata lakshmi—for being part of my journey to this point.

Finally, and most importantly, I thank all my role models —Sandeep Maheshwari, Robert Greene, Steve Jobs, Leonardo Da Vinci, Picasso, Yoshihiro Togashi, Deep Trivedi, Jeremy Wang, Ram Gopal Varma, and Daniel Naroditsky—who, even though I have never met them, are my mentors. I have learned a great deal from them through their online videos, books, and movies.

THE SUNRISE IS MISSING

CHAPTER 1

"Darsh, come quickly. Your breakfast is ready." I heard my Mom shout while I was getting ready.

"Yes Mom, I will be there in 2 minutes," I said.

Today I had my 7th-grade class field trip. I couldn't sleep last night because of the excitement of going on a field trip. I kept wondering about what would happen and how fun it would be to enjoy with friends all day. I went to a grocery shop yesterday evening and bought all my favourite snacks to eat on the bus.

I was also feeling anxious because this would be my first time being far away from home. I wore my shirt inside out – the mistake I always make when I am nervous. I took off my shirt and put it on again, and this time it was correct. Today, I wore my favourite green T-shirt and black pants.

I finished my breakfast, waved good-bye to Mom, and left the house.

The weather was strange – the clouds hid the sun. I continued walking to my school. I saw one of my friends at a distance, waving his hand. It was Anitosh. I ran towards him.

Anitosh wore a tight yellow T-shirt with light brown pants and brown shoes. He has thick hair and eyebrows and he's a little shorter than me. He was also skinny, just like me.

"Hey Darsh, are you excited about today's trip?" Anitosh asked.

"Very much!"

"The weather isn't great today," Anitosh said with a very sad tone.

"It's okay, the weather will be alright by the time we reach our destination."

We walked until we reached the main gate of the school. The guard instructed us to get inside the building as the bus had arrived. We jogged into the school and went to the playground with all our classmates. I study in a government school which consists of 60 students. Only 36 students had enrolled for the field trip – out of which 26 were boys and 10 were girls. All of us were showing each other the snacks, shoes, mobile phones, and the other cool items they brought for the field trip.

"What snacks did you get, Darsh?" Anitosh asked.

"All my favorite stuff, I will show you after boarding the bus." I said.

Our principal and two of our teachers came to the playground and asked us to stand in a queue. The bus that was going to take us to our destination had just entered the playground. The bus was newly painted in a pink color with the name of our school written on the sides, but it's lower part was extremely dirty with mud. Our teachers instructed us to get on the bus one by one. All the students screamed with excitement once everyone settled.

The bus had a metal seat structure and the cushion of the bus was blue. The students got onto the bus while the teachers and the driver were talking on the playground. I sat beside Anitosh in the second to last seat and there was no one behind us. The seats weren't very comfortable. The bus was very dark inside. The interior seemed very old with a lot of stickers and scorches. We were waiting for the bus to start.

Gradually, the clouds got thicker and thicker, blocking all the sunlight. I had never seen the sky as cloudy as this before.

"Seems like the weather is getting worse." Anitosh said.

I nodded.

Then it started to rain.

The wind picked up significantly. The windows of the bus began to rattle due to the wind. The trees outside started shaking, bending to the wind. It seemed like they were about to break and fall on the bus. The boys who were seated at the front of the bus kept shouting as the speed of the wind kept increasing.

It begun to rain. It hadn't rained in our town for ages. I felt frustrated that it had to rain on the day we had our field trip. Then we heard the sound of a thunderstorm, which gave us chills. It wasn't a normal thunderstorm. It felt very intense. The boys stopped screaming. Everyone were shocked and chills ran down their spines as they listened to the sounds of thunderstorms. The weather was turning bad very rapidly.

"Is the field trip going to get cancelled?" asked Anitosh, looking outside. He sounded very disappointed and worried.

"I hope not," I said.

The thunderstorms started increasing. It grew as dark as night, while the clouds covered the entire sun. All we could see outside was the rain. Although we closed the bus windows, all the students were shivering due to the cold wind.

"It's a tsunami" one of the students shouted on the bus. Everyone screamed.

"It had to come today out of all the days." A student shouted and then groaned. I thought the same.

"I just want to go home now." Anitosh cried out.

One of our teachers entered the bus with an umbrella and shouted, "Students, the field trip stands canceled due to the violent weather. Please stay on the bus until the weather's cleared."

All the students groaned in disappointment. A very intense lightning bolt struck a few meters in front of the bus. The sound of the storm gave everyone chills, including the teacher on the bus.

CHAPTER 2

Over 10 minutes passed and the clouds started to move away. The rays of the sunlight came out. The thunderstorm stopped. The weather gradually got back to normal. It was still a little windy but not as much as before.

We pleaded the teacher to resume the field trip as the weather was clearing up. The teacher instructed us to wait while she got off the bus and walked towards the other teachers who were in the discussion room.

We all celebrated as the weather got back to normal. Anitosh and all the other students looked very happy sharing all the stuff they planned for the trip.

Mr. Prasad, our principal, who was tall with a thick moustache, entered the bus.

"Sir, will the trip resume?" One student in front pleaded.

"If the weather gets better by 20 minutes, the trip will resume back." The principal smiled.

All the students cheered. We hoped the weather would remain the same.

20 minutes passed by and now it was a bright sunny day. It didn't seem like it rained a while ago.

The bus driver slipped into his seat, The teachers entered the bus. All of us smiled and laughed. Boys kept shouting and having fun while the girls were talking amongst themselves. One of our teachers, our physical trainer teacher, Prakash, invited Anitosh to the front, as our class leader was absent. There was a little work that needed to be done, and Anitosh was a sincere student.

Anitosh sat beside the teacher. He said sorry to me before moving and now I sat alone in my seat. I was sad because I wouldn't be able to share my snacks with anyone now. The bus started to move. Leaving my town and home behind made me nervous again. Everyone had a partner to sit with except for me. The boys were dancing and singing on the bus, while the girls watched the boys dance, sometimes ignoring them and sometimes smiling at them. The bus driver constantly shouted at the boys to get back to their seats but sometimes smiled looking at them having fun.

We were going to a little adventure park that was very far from our village. We had to travel through a forest for a long time to reach our destination.

I looked out of the window as the bus moved. All I could see was trees. It was very dark in the woods. I could see green mountains at a distance. I felt someone staring at me. It felt like someone was moving into the woods alongside the bus.

A hand grabbed my shoulder from behind.

CHAPTER 3

I was startled, there was no one sitting behind me. I turned around.

Was he a new student? I had never seen him before at the school.

"Hello, I am Raghav!" He introduced himself in an excited voice.

"Hey." I was breathless because I was shocked to see someone behind me.

He had a huge smile on his face.

"Why don't you come and sit beside me?" He asked.

I asked if he wanted to come up and sit beside me. He insisted that I sit beside him on the opposite side of the bus. I moved back and sat where he said. Raghav was wearing a white t-shirt and black pants with brown slippers. He had a scar on the right side of his forehead. It looked like an animal scratch with three different lines, the middle one being longer than the others.

He kept staring at me. His look creeped me out. He kept staring at my eyes and forehead.

"I am going to kill you now," He said and grabbed my neck.

I screamed.

He laughed at me.

"It was just a joke." He said and kept laughing.

Not a lot of people heard my scream, even though I screamed at the top of my lungs. The people who did hear me looked back at us. I smiled and they returned back to minding their business.

"Do you study in this school?" I asked him.

"No, I am the bus driver's son, I tagged along with my dad because my Mum is not at home," He said while smiling.

"What's your age?" I asked him out of curiosity.

"14." He replied.

"I am 13, and my name is Darsh."

"How did you get that scar on your face?" I asked him

"Oh, this? It's a long story. I will tell you during our way back from the trip." He said.

He had a very weird watch on his wrist, it was golden and black coated. "Can I look at your watch?" I asked him.

"Yes, sure. You can keep it till the end of the trip." He said.

I took the watch and put it on. It was a very heavy watch but It looked very luxurious and classic.

"Is this a vintage watch?" I asked him.

"Yes, it's a very very old watch." He said.

"I am happy that you are joining us for the trip," I said.

"Yes, this is my first ever trip!" He exclaimed.

"Your first?" I asked, surprised.

"Yes, I haven't been on a trip before." He said.

"You must be very excited." I said

"Yes, very." He said with a huge smile.

We talked about the trip for a while until I heard his stomach growling. I opened up my bag and shared my snacks with him. At first, he hesitated but eventually, he accepted. He also shared his snacks with me. We kept talking about what we were going to do when we reached the park.

Then we heard a huge explosion and the bus stopped.

CHAPTER 4

A few students shouted while the others wondered what went wrong. The teachers and the bus driver headed outside the bus. The bus was tilted a little towards the left.

Mr. Prakash, our physical trainer teacher, got back on the bus.

"Students, one of the bus tires is punctured, so I need everyone off the bus now." He said.

All the students groaned.

"It's not our day today," I told Raghav while getting off the bus. He nodded.

We all got off in the middle of the woods. There were no other vehicles or people on the road. All of us stood in a group outside of the bus.

One of the students went to our principal and said that he had to pee. He and the principal went into the woods. The bus driver took a new bus tire out of the trunk and began to replace it with the punctured one.

I felt that someone was watching us over from the woods. I turned my head and saw nothing but trees. A lot of boys needed to pee but teachers instructed them not to go anywhere until the principal was back. I saw a huge tree standing opposite to us which had multiple curves. A lot of trees had weird stripes on them and most of them were curved in shape. It was my first time seeing trees with so many curves. I stood next to Raghav. He kept smiling while everyone else was angry and kept complaining about how unlucky we were.

The teacher assigned Anitosh the task of ensuring that all the kids were in a group and no one is lost.

A fight broke out between two students as they kept shouting and teasing each other. Hearing the commotion, Mr. Prakash went to stop them and asked the reason for the fight. Both kept blaming each other.

"They fought over a biscuit." a student said. Everyone laughed.

The teacher scolded them.

Then we heard a scream from the woods. The scream was louder than a lion's roar. It was a scream of terror.

Both teachers looked at each other. Some students took a step back toward the teachers.

We saw the guy who went to pee with the principal alone. The principal wasn't with him.

"Where is the principal?" Mr. Prakash asked in a worrisome voice.

The student didn't utter a word. He started signing. His eyes became big and he was shivering.

"Where did the principal go?" Mr. Prakash asked again.

He kept humming but he couldn't open his mouth.

CHAPTER 5

Teachers screamed at us, asking us to go back to the bus. Some students screamed while the others cried out as they ran towards the bus. I was very frightened.

Then the principal emerged from the woods, adjusting his pants. The teachers sighed when they saw him.

I laughed thinking about how easy it was to be scared in an unknown place.

"The bus is ready to go." We heard the bus driver shout from the road. All of us entered the bus.

The teachers gathered all the students and took a head count. Anitosh counted as well. Anitosh is a very sincere student, and all the teachers like him very much.

Everyone came back to their seats, while I sat in the back corner seat with Raghav. I started to like Raghav, he smiled a lot. He has a very big smile.

The bus started up again and our journey resumed. Everyone cheered.

Students played music on their phones and danced. Teachers looked at them attempting to calm them down, but at times just smiled.

I still felt like someone was watching us from the woods. It felt like someone was following us.

Raghav and I talked about our school life.

The bus driver applied the brake without a sign which made all the students, including me, jump off our seats.

CHAPTER 6

We saw a huge sign in front of us: Dream Water Adventure Park.

All the students cheered as they saw this. We reached the park! All I wanted to do was to get off the bus and start enjoying myself. It was a very long and strange ride. It's time we enjoy, I thought.

Teachers instructed everyone to get off the bus. Everyone got off and started walking towards the entrance of the park. It had a huge entrance. The staff members were standing outside to greet our teachers. I wasn't expecting our school to organize such a nice trip. It was above my expectations.

Raghav and I were walking behind everyone. Anitosh turned around and started running back towards the bus.

"Where are you going?" I asked him.

"I forgot my water bottle!" He said.

"Go and get it fast, it's time to have fun," I said with a bright smile on my face.

"Yes, yes one minute," He said and started running towards the bus.

Raghav and I kept walking but I asked Raghav to slow down. I wanted to wait for Anitosh.

"Here we are finally, Raghav. How do you feel?" I asked him, looking

back to the bus. I didn't get a reply.

I turned and looked to my left, but he wasn't there. I assumed he went ahead. Raghav must be excited about his very first trip. I walked very slowly, waiting for Anitosh.

I heard a scream. I looked back and saw Anitosh running toward me. Some students stopped and looked, but some didn't care and kept walking to the front gate which was much farther than it looked. The sun was on top of us. It was the hottest day. How did the weather change so quickly, I wondered. I don't usually sweat but this heat is even making me hot.

Anitosh started running towards me.

"Darsh! Darsh! I saw a ghost on the bus!" He said breathlessly in terror.

"It might just be your imagination, Anitosh. The heat of the sun sometimes causes an illusion."

"No Darsh, I saw my shadow move on its own. Please, let's run to our teachers" He cried out.

" You are thinking too much due to the excitement and heat Anitosh," I assured him and

asked him to drink water.

He relaxed a little and we ran up to my friends while entering the park. I looked back at the bus one last time before entering the gate.

CHAPTER 7

It was one of the best field trips of my life.

We enjoyed the park and started going back to the bus. All the students were exhausted now. There was no jumping and shouting. I was at peace too.

I sat in the corner seat but Raghav wasn't seated beside me. I thought he was sitting in the front with someone else, but I was too tired to go and check on him. I played a lot of games in the park like Kabaddi, cricket, and volleyball. My legs felt like noodles. It felt like needles going into every part of my leg.

I looked out through the bus window. It was a wonderful evening view. The clouds were orange and the sun was about to set between the hills.

I forgot about all the weird things that happened earlier in the morning. The night would be falling any moment now.

All the students were listening to music, with their earphones on.

I was tired and wanted to sleep. I remembered that I didn't sleep last night either. I closed my eyes for some time.

I heard that same explosive sound again – the same sound I heard in the morning. The bus tilted again to the left side.

All the students got up from their seats and sighed. The teachers and drivers exchanged looks.

The teachers and the bus driver got out to see if the tire was punctured again. Mr. Prakash came into the bus and asked if anyone needed to pee.

"Students, if you want to pee, do it now as there will be no more stops in the darkness."

The students got off. I thought about not getting off because I already peed at the park, but still got off because I didn't know when the chance might come again and I didn't want to risk it.

I got off the bus and went to the woods to complete the task for which I was born.

I got back on the bus because I wanted to eat the snack that I had forgotten about. I wanted to get that snack into my pocket as soon as possible. When I got back on the bus, I saw 3 people there: Anitosh, Rishitha, & Supriya. I went to the back and saw that my snack was still in my bag.

I didn't know what was going to happen. I just saw the teachers and drivers talking. I didn't even care too much because all I wanted to do was to eat my snack.

Anitosh called me up to the front. I went up and started talking with them. We talked about our experiences on the field trip and the games we played. All the other students were talking outside, making noises, and taking pictures.

Then two more boys entered the bus, Nitish and Rahul. They were both laughing. They came near Anitosh and screamed at him, trying to make him scared.

"Do you think this is fun?" I shouted at them.

"Yes, of course." said Rahul while laughing.

Rishitha and Supriya turned in the opposite direction.

"How are you, Supriyaaaa?" They said, making fun of her.

"It's not appropriate to talk like that," I said again in a very high pitch.

"What are you going to do about it, Darsh? Do you dare to fight?" Nitish asked sarcastically.

They kept laughing. I stopped hearing the sounds of talking from outside. All I could hear were their laughs.

"Guys, why did everyone outside go silent?" I asked.

"Yes, it became quiet all of a sudden." Anitosh replied.

Antosh and I immediately looked through the window and saw no one. Supriya and Rishitha looked through the opposite window and said there was no one there either.

CHAPTER 8

Chills ran up my spine when Rishitha and Supriya said that.

"Let's go outside and check." Rahul suggested with terror and shock in his eyes.

"Yes," I replied.

Me, Rahul, and Nitish went outside and started shouting the names of our friends.

"Prakash sir!"

"Principal sir!"

"Ashish!"

We kept shouting while moving around the bus. Supriya, Rishitha, and Anitosh also got off the bus. We saw no one and heard nothing from the trees shaking in the wind. We were on a road with no sound other than our footsteps and voices. With every step we were taking, I could hear my heartbeat going fast and faster. I couldn't even believe what was happening.

"What happened? Where are they?" Rishitha asked as we completed a rotation of the bus.

"No one is out there, not a single soul." I said, my voice breaking due to the

chills. My heart was pounding.

Everyone cried out.

"What do you mean no one is there?" Anitosh asked, crying.

"There is no one." Rahul said, with his eyes wide open.

"How's that even possible?"

"It's better to get on the bus." Rishitha suggested.

We all got back on the bus.

"It's impossible, how come there is no one outside?" Anitosh cried out.

I didn't understand how this was even possible. They all went missing without a sound. Is this just a bad dream, I thought. The last thing I remembered was taking a nap. I asked Nitish to pinch me. He didn't seem to understand.

"This is not time for a joke," Supriya said seriously and cried out.

Anitosh stepped on my leg and it pained me. This was not a dream. It was happening.

"Let's close the windows and the doors of the bus, a lot of mosquitos are coming in." Rishitha said. She was braver and wiser than all of us.

Each one of us started closing the windows of the bus. I went to the front and pressed the button which closed the door of the bus. We felt a little safe.

"What could have even happened? I don't understand anything." Anitosh cried out.

As I was at the front of the bus, I was looking at the road and saw a shadow moving in front of us. I screamed.

CHAPTER 9

"What happened?" Anitosh asked with terror on his face.

"Nothing, I just don't understand anything," I said. I didn't want to terrorize them anymore. It might be just my imagination.

"People can't just disappear into thin air without a sound," Rahul said.

"But what even happened?" Anitosh Stammered.

Our voices kept on breaking because of the terror and we all were shivering. The cold wind of the night started to get stronger.

Rishitha kept checking her phone but she had no signal. She asked all of us to check if any of the mobiles has a signal so that we can call someone for help. I went back to my seat and checked my small mobile and saw that it also doesn't have any signal. None of our phones had any signals.

It was getting dark outside. The sun was almost about to set.

"It's getting dark. How do we get out of here?" Anitosh cried out.

"We have to figure out a way to find our friends and teachers and get out of here," said Rishitha.

"Yes, let's sit down and find out a solution," I stammered while my heart raced.

"I think we have to turn on the bus' headlights," Nitish said nervously.

I went to the front and turned the headlight knob while my hands were shaking. This time I didn't see the road. It was kind of eerie, just 6 people in the middle of the woods, and everyone else disappeared. My throat started to feel dry.

"Are we stuck in the middle of the woods?" Anitosh asked

"I hope not." Said Supriya.

We were all trying to figure out what could have happened.

"Could this be a prank?" Anitosh asked.

"No, why would they prank us and how would they just disappear?" Supriya declared.

"Maybe, they just want to make fun of us." Rahul stammered.

Rahul opened the window and shouted "Okay guys, you scared us. Now, please come back to the bus." It was dead silent outside. It kept getting darker. The sun was about to set. Only a few rays of sunlight were falling and they would be gone in just a few minutes.

Nitish also kept shouting through the window and still couldn't believe what was happening. Rishitha kept trying to find a signal to her phone, moving it all over the bus. Anitosh just closed his eyes and cried. Supriya also closed her eyes and prayed. I was in a state of shock trying to understand what could have happened.

It got completely dark outside. The bus had a light inside but it was broken. The only light we were relying on now was the bus headlights.

"Are we also going to disappear now?" Supriya asked.

"Should we go a little into the woods and search for our friends?" Rahul asked.

"No, we will stay on the bus till we understand what's happened." Rishitha said.

"Hey guys, look. The headlights are blinking." Anitosh shouted with terror.

We all looked forward, at the blinking headlights. At one moment, we couldn't see anything, and the next moment we saw the road. Then the headlights turned off completely.

CHAPTER 10

The headlights were completely off, making it very dark. Everyone on the bus screamed for help.

"Help us!"

"Help us!"

"Help us!" Rahul kept shouting.

The headlights started blinking again. It was the most horrifying thing I had ever seen. I was thinking about the shadow that passed by us before. Was it real or was it just my imagination? I hope it doesn't happen again.

With a lot of courage, I went to the front of the bus again and turned the headlight knob a few times.

The headlight went back to normal. We all sighed a little, but deep within we were very terrorized.

"I don't think we should waste our time thinking about how they disappeared. We should focus on escaping and reaching a safe place." said Rishitha.

"But they are our friends. We need to find them." Anitosh stammered.

"We will only be able to find them if we escape from here and get more people to help us," Rishitha said.

"But how? How are we going to escape?" Supriya asked weakly.

"We need to figure that out," Rishitha said.

No one dared to even look out the window. It was completely dark outside. We all were seated in the 2nd and 3rd rows of the bus. We made a circle sitting on the seats.

A foul smell started to spread through the bus, even with the windows closed.

"Eww, what is this smell?" Anitosh asked breathlessly. The smell kept getting stronger.

The smell made it difficult for us to breathe.

We saw a light falling on us, we turned our heads to see a car coming toward us. We looked at each other.

"They could help us!" Rahul said. He ran to the front and pressed the button to open the door and went out.

"Wait—" Rishitha shouted but couldn't complete what she wanted to say.

All of us ran out of the bus.

"Wave your hands!" Rahul said.

We started waving our hands at the car. It passed us and the bus. We kept shouting.

The car stopped. We all ran towards it. Rahul knocked on the window. We saw a young couple inside. They kept shaking as they got out. They smelled like they were drunk. They kept smiling very weirdly while looking at each other. The man wore a very weird hat and a shirt with flowers on it and black pants. The woman wore a pink T-shirt and jeans.

"Hey, we need your help!"

"We lost our friends in the woods!"

"Does your mobile have a signal to make a call?"

"Did you see anyone coming from that direction?"

We bombarded them with multiple questions.

The couple kept looking at each other and smiling.

"Be quiet!" The man shouted but kept smiling.

"Sir, you have to understand our situation. We are missing our friends and teachers. We need to find them and also get to our village. It's not safe in the woods at night." said Rishitha.

They both laughed out loud.

"Is this a new prank or are you kids trying to steal from us?" The man said.

His wife kept laughing.

"Poor kids, they are lost it seems." The woman said.

Rahul grabbed the man's hand.

"This is not funny, we are lost. Why don't you understand the seriousness of this situation?" Rahul said in a very angry tone.

"Lost? Where are your other friends kids? Isn't the prank over yet?" The man said.

"We are not going to get played by your tricks," The woman said.

"Look around, we don't have anyone here. They disappeared." I said to them.

"Dis— Disappeared?" The man said and they laughed even louder.

Rahul kept grabbing his hand and made a very serious and angry face.

The man got very irritated because of Rahul and gave him a spooky smile.

"It's time for you guys to burn," The man said in a very rough voice.

CHAPTER 11

Rahul immediately let go of his hand. He was very frightened. So was everyone else.

"Honey, don't joke around. They are just poor kids." The woman said.

They both started laughing again.

Some joke it was.

We were all very angry that they did not understand the intensity of our problem.

Nitish shouted at them "Listen carefully. We were coming back from our field trip. The tire of our bus got punctured, as you can see, and then our friends got off the bus and then they disappeared."

They both laughed.

"Do you think we would fall for that?" The man said.

"How did your friends disappear?" The woman asked.

"We don't know!" We all shouted at them at once.

It started to rain.

"Let's get on the bus, quickly." I said "Please get on the bus with us. We need your help. " I said to the couple.

"Why don't you guys get in our car? Or better, why don't you guys leave your way, and we'll leave ours?" The man said

"You need to come with us, please. Eight people won't fit in your car. Let's find a solution to this on the bus." Anitosh said in his stammering voice.

It went from drizzling to heavy rain very quickly.

They stopped laughing and I guess they started to see fear in our eyes. They agreed to get on the bus.

We invited strangers into our bus. I knew it was a very dangerous idea to invite strangers on, but we were already in so much danger, we didn't have any other choice.

We closed the door. The couple was still smiling, but shaking.

"Can you check if your mobile has a signal to make a call?" Rishitha asked the couple as soon as they entered the bus.

"Why? Are you going to rob our phones?" The man said, grinning.

"No, just check if you have a signal," said Rahul.

The man got his phone out.

"No signal, kids. Why would there even be a signal this far in the woods" He laughed again.

"Oh no, I left my handbag in the car." The woman said.

"Good thing honey, now they can't steal it, " The man said and laughed. We sighed.

"All right, let's make a plan now," I said.

The foul smell kept increasing in the bus.

"What is this smell, where is it coming from?" Supriya asked.

The bus headlights started blinking again. I looked back and the headlights of the car also turned off completely.

"Why did it happen again?" Anitosh stammered.

Both the adults saw the blinking lights and screamed.

"Can you please go and turn the knob again?" Rahul asked in terror.

I didn't want to. My legs were shaking. I was breathless. I asked the man if he could do it but he was also shaking. The woman covered her face with her hands.

I went to the front of the bus and the headlights turned off completely.

Everyone screamed in terror. A chill ran through my body. I was able to hear my heart beating.

I kept turning the knob, closing one eye, and looking down with fear. Even after trying more than 5 times. The headlights were still completely off and didn't show a sign on turning on again.

CHAPTER 12

I ran towards my friends. We were in complete darkness and all we could hear was the tiny droplets of rain falling outside. We couldn't see anything around our bus.

That darkness, silence, and foul smell gave me chills all over my body.

"Do something, do something!" The man and wife cried out.

Someone wrapped their fingers around my wrist very tightly.

"Darsh, please keep holding my hand." Anitosh cried out.

Nitish and Rahul kept screaming and holding each other. Supriya turned herself into the seat while a hand of hers was on Rishitha.

Rishitha closed her eyes and was shivering.

We heard someone walking above our bus. We all looked up. It sounds like an animal with big claws. We could hear the sound moving from the back toward the front.

Everyone opened their eyes.

"Am I the only one hearing it?" Anitosh asked in terror.

Rishitha put her finger to her lips and signaled all of us to keep quiet. The couple stood still. They screamed.

"Shhh" I signaled to them.

"Who is that walking on top of the bus?" Nitish shouted.

"Who is it?" Rahul shouted.

The sounds stopped right above us. We could hear very loud breathing from the top of the bus. The foul smell kept increasing making it hard for us to breathe.

Everyone held their noses with one hand and their lips with another. We kept looking at each other.

I didn't know if being quiet was the right thing to do. We still kept hearing heavy breathing from above.

Anitosh started crying. Everyone else, including me, started to sweat a lot.

The sounds of crawling started again. The sounds were passed over to the front of the bus. We closed one eye and watched the front of the bus with the other. Anitosh closed both his eyes. I felt very bad seeing him in terror.

We heard the roof of the bus being scratched and saw a hand on the window of the bus. The hand was big with huge claws. The blood on the hand dripped down the window. The hand looked like a tiger's. But with a lot of scratches on it, it was much scarier than a tiger's claw.

Anitosh opened his eyes and saw the creature's hand and went unconscious. I screamed and then everyone screamed.

Another hand appeared in the window. The blood was now dripping from both the hands.

CHAPTER 13

The headlights of the bus turned on again. The hand pulled away from the window and the footsteps ran towards the back of the bus and then we could no longer hear them.

I sighed in relief. What even is happening? I thought.

The foul smell slowly started to fade away.

I looked back only to see both the adults wet their pants.

The rain also slowly decreased.

The couple opened their eyes wide and sat on the 4th seat.

"It's the red-eyed creature of the Gaha," The man said shivering. I could see he was very terrified.

"What? Red-eyed creature?" I said.

Everyone's eyes were open and everyone had goosebumps on their skin.

"What is Red-eyed—?" Supriya stammered.

"Red-eyed creature of the Gaha woods," The man said while opening his eyes wide.

"Is this another joke of yours?" Rishitha asked.

"No, no. The Red-eyed creature of the Gaha. It is said to be a creature that lives in the Gaha woods." The man said with a fearsome voice.

"What does it — do?" Supriya asked with dread and fear in her eyes.

"It's said that the Red-eyed creature of the Gaha eats humans," The man stammered.

"Eat??" I gasped.

Everyone on the bus started breathing faster when they heard this.

"Yes, the Red-eyed creature of Gaha eats humans. Since 20 years, there have been many rumors and stories about it." The man said.

"What kind of rumors? What are those stories?" I asked.

"In the past, there were many people who entered the Gaha woods and disappeared into thin air. No one understood the reason for their disappearance. One day a group of men went into the Gaha forest to search for the source of this problem. While searching for those men, they found a creature. A red-eyed creature. They thought that it was the reason for all the mysterious disappearances. I always thought it was just a rumor or a story created by the villagers to bring in fear. But to—today, I saw it with my own eyes" The man said and screamed.

Everyone on the bus got chills when the man narrated this story. Anitosh was still unconscious. I thought it would be best for him to sleep rather than listen to these stories as would make him more afraid. I checked his pulse for safety and he was alive. He was just in a deep sleep.

"Do you think that one creature ate all of our friends and teachers? Rishitha asked, looking into the eyes of the man.

Rishitha never trusts any rumors or stories. She always believes in questioning everything. I always thought that she is one of the most intelligent students in the school.

"I don't know — Maybe." The man said with a confused and low voice.

"Impossible," Rishitha said.

I thought the same. It would be impossible for a single creature to eat all of our friends and teachers and none of them made a sound. We would have immediately known if someone got attacked.

"Okay, so — How do we escape from the creature?" Supriya asked in a low crackling voice.

"I don't know, but it's been said that once the Red-eyed creature lays its eyes on someone or something and it won't let go of it until it gets that. And will go to any extent to get it." The man said.

We all heard a howl, a howl that kept echoing in the woods.

CHAPTER 14

On the bus, everyone was sweating. There was no airflow whatsoever.

I would hear the continuous breathing of all my friends. They all looked very tense. Rahul folded his hands. Supriya held her seat very tightly. I was sitting in front of Rishitha, pressing myself to the seat. I looked at Raghav's watch and it was broken. I was sad to see such a good watch broken.

"But there might be one way to escape from it," The man said with a little excitement.

"What is it?" Rahul asked in his frightened voice.

We all started getting a little closer to the man.

"When the sun rises, we can escape from it as there are no missing reports or cases in the daytime. Only the sunrise can save us now." The man said.

" Great— all we have is to stay safe till the morning," Rahul said. His voice kept going down while he was saying this.

The headlights of the bus turned off again. We looked at each other in the darkness.

"Uh-oh," I said.

"Make sure you guys whisper when you talk." Rishitha whispered.

"It won't help us get rid of the creature," The man said

"Sir, please whisper." Rahul whispered.

We heard hissing sounds. We focused on where the sound came from. The sound came from the back of the bus.

"What is that sound?" Supriya whispered.

The hissing sound became louder. It kept on coming closer. Everyone on the bus was profoundly sweating, The sounds came nearer and nearer.

The hissing sound came near my legs. I looked down and saw that it was a mouse.

"It's just a mouse!" I shouted in excitement. I've always been scared when I saw a mice in my home or

school, but seeing a mouse in the woods is so much better.

All the students tried to signal me to be silent and Rishitha signalled me to try turning the headlight knob on.

"Why do I always have to go?" I asked, furious. "Why don't you guys go?"

I looked at the man "Can you turn on the nob?" I asked him.

He couldn't move his legs.

"No — no. I don't know how to. I would have done it but it's just I don't know how to." He said. " Please turn on the headlights, please go fast," He said with a tense voice.

It's my duty again, I thought. I looked out the window. The road was in complete darkness. I saw the moonlight falling on the roof and the trees. I saw the shadows of the trees falling on the road which made the road appear even darker. I went forward.

I saw the most beautiful full moon of my life. The stars covered the entire sky. It was my first time seeing that clear sky. It was to be remembered for life.

"What are you doing? Turn on the headlights quickly!" Rahul whispered.

I turned the knob again, again, and again. Nothing. No headlights. I looked back and moved my head from side to side, signaling that I couldn't turn on the headlights.

All my friends gasped. I went a little forward to look for loose wire connections of the headlights. I kept checking all the wires. I used my phone's torch.

I found it. Two wires were loosely connected by transparent tape.

"What are you still doing? Come back here, Darsh." Rahul whispered again.

I moved the wire a little and the headlights blinked. It was an instant blink, but it was easy to notice in that complete darkness. I tried to connect both wires stiffly and the headlights turned on.

I celebrated. I looked back with a happy smile. Everyone on the bus was impressed and happy.

"Awesome!" Rishitha whispered.

"Yes, Darsh, amazing!" Rahul whispered.

"Yes, yes." Supriya whispered, her smile wide.

"Why are we still whispering?" The man asked.

"It's better to whisper. It feels safer in these woods to whisper," I said.

All my friends nodded.

"All we have to do is to stay safe till the morning and stay together and we will get out of here. Then we can find our friends and help them," I said with excitement.

Everyone nodded.

I sat down and relaxed. It was a crazy day. I hoped the night passed quickly. I hoped that I could just close my eyes, wake up, and see the daylight.

My legs are hurting. They felt like an iron hammer was constantly hitting them. I felt sleepy so I closed my eyes. I opened them again. I wanted to be awake all night to keep my friends protected. I closed my eyes again. I felt very good to just keep my eyes closed but I opened them again and thought I would be awake all night.

When I looked back, I saw everyone's eyes closed and leaned back to their seats. I took my water bottle and drank some water and just thought to close my eyes for a little while.

I closed my eyes.

I heard someone whispering behind me. I didn't want to open my eyes, but I still kept hearing the whispers from behind. Someone was whispering my name. The sound of the whisper was like an old lady whispering my name and the whisper kept on coming. Each time increasing the exaggeration in my name.

"Darsh."

"Dar-shh."

"Daaar-sshh."

I opened my eyes and looked back and there was no one whispering my name. Everyone was asleep. I got up from my seat and saw that there was no one whispering my name. I thought it was just my imagination. I thought I just needed a little sleep. I drank water again. I took a few breaths in. I closed my eyes again. Someone grabbed my shoulder from behind.

CHAPTER 15

I closed my eyes again and slept. Someone grabbed my shoulder from behind.

"Wake up Darsh, wake up." someone whispered while shaking my shoulders.

I opened my eyes and immediately looked back.

It was Rahul. He pointed towards the front of the bus.

"Look Darsh, the headlights turned off again." He whispered.

I saw headlights were off and the road was in complete darkness. I started to get a headache due to no proper sleep. It was like someone was pulling my head away from me.

"Okay wait, let me turn them on." I whispered with exhaustion and went to the front of the bus with my phone torch on. I kept searching for the wire but couldn't find it. I just wanted to sleep peacefully. I could find every other wire except for the headlights wire. All of my other friends were having a peaceful sleep.

"What's taking so long?" Rahul whispered from behind.

"I can't find the wire." I whispered.

"What do you mean you can find it? Search faster!" he whispered.

He was sitting down holding the seat very tightly.

I found the wire. I pressed it hard again. The headlights still didn't turn on. I tried turning the wires in different directions but still, the headlights didn't turn on.

"Please do it fast." Rahul whispered

"Wait, I am trying my best." I whispered back to him.

I kept trying to turn the wires, pressing them hard. The headlights still didn't turn on. I pressed and pushed a little hard. The two wires which were connected instantly got disconnected.

I looked at it with fear. I looked through the window and back to the wires. I kept trying to connect without tape but all the efforts went in vain. The headlights won't turn on.

"The wires are broken." I whispered to Rahul.

He gasped. He opened his eyes wide open with fear. He opened his mouth very wide. He was in shock.

"Don't scream" I whispered. I went back to him.

"Just sleep now, we don't need the headlights" I whispered to him.

"I can't sleep in the dark, especially after what happened." He whispered.

I understood his concern. I didn't know if I would be able to sleep peacefully without the headlights. I I asked him to put on his torchlight, so that there is enough light to radiate across the bus along with the moonlight which fell on the ground of the bus and reflected on the entire bus. It wasn't as dark as before.

"Good idea, let me turn on my phone's torch." Rahul whispered.

He looked backward.

"Come with me to my bag Darsh, my bag is on the third seat from behind." Rahul whispered.

"Why didn't you bring your bag to the front before?" I whispered.

"How could I? I couldn't even take two steps." He whispered.

"Okay, let's go." I whispered.

We started going backward on the bus. I was using my torch to navigate through the path. We walked slowly. Rahul was in front of me so I held the torch for a better visibility of what was ahead.

We reached for his bag. He grabbed his bag and ran in front, leaving me behind. He ran like he was in a world cup race.

"Come fast." Rahul whispered and ran.

I looked at him and started walking towards him. I heard another whisper immediately after that. It was a very faint whisper which was coming from behind. The sound of the whisper kept increasing as I took each breath.

"Daaarrshhh," Someone whispered behind me with the same old lady's voice. I didn't want to turn back now so I ran quickly towards Rahul.

"Take out your phone," I whispered to Rahul.

Rahul took out his phone and turned on the flashlight. Now we had two flashlights on the bus.

"Should I wake our friends up and ask them to turn on their flashlights too?" Rahul whispered to me.

"No, let them rest. Two is enough for now. You go to sleep. I will be awake and make sure we are safe." I whispered.

"Really?" Rahul asked.

"Yes, You can sleep peacefully and leave the night duty to me." I reassured him.

"Thank you, Darsh." Rahul whispered and sat down beside Nitish and closed his eyes. I went up to Anitosh and sat beside him.

I wondered what to do. I had nothing to do but keep an eye out all night when I was very sleepy. Anyone could easily guess that I was sleepy looking into my eyes. I leaned my body towards the seat and my eyes closed.

And we heard it again, what we were afraid of the most; the footsteps of the creature on top of the bus.

CHAPTER 16

It was so loud that everyone woke up from their sleep, even Anitosh woke up and started shouting.

"Help, help!" Anitosh kept shouting as soon as he woke up.

We signaled him to stay calm. The woman stood up and was holding up her hand high while the man was holding back his wife, bending down behind her and catching her shoulders.

We heard footsteps coming from behind. The foul smell came back again. We all kept watching the back of the bus.

"I just want to go home. I just want to go home." Rahul screamed.

We signalled him to be quiet. The footsteps started to come forward.

"Everyone take out your phones and turn on your torch lights!" I whispered out loud.

Everyone started to search for their phone, in their bag and pockets. The creature kept coming forward. We could hear the breath of the creature as it was stepping near us. The creature's breathing kept getting intense as it was coming slower.

Everyone took their phones and started the torch lights on their phones.

"Point it towards the front window when the creature steps on the window." I whispered.

The creature stepped a little forward. A little more. All of our eyes were following the sound of the creature.

"Why?" Anitosh asked.

"Because last time when the headlights turned on, the creature ran away. Maybe it's afraid of the light. It's our only shot now." I said.

The footsteps started coming from right above us. We kept looking up. The footsteps got to the front of the bus.

The foot of the creature got on the bus window.

"Now!" I screamed.

Everyone pointed their torch lights towards the bus window and the creature took his foot back and stepped to the end of the bus.

We celebrated.

"Yes!" Rahul cheered up.

"We figured it out"

"Great observation." Rishitha said.

A compliment from her made me even happier. I was happy that we could send off that creature but I realized that I couldn't sleep anymore.

We heard the sound of glass cracking from behind. We looked behind.

The creature entered the bus by breaking the side window.

CHAPTER 17

The creature entered the bus from the side window.

"Oh-no," The man shouted.

Everyone on the bus screamed at the top of their lungs.

I saw the creature right in front of me. It had bright red eyes which were surrounded by a glass-like structure. The creature was 3ft. tall. It had the biggest claws I had ever seen and its teeth were covered with fresh blood.

I ran towards the front of the bus as soon as I saw the creature and pressed the button to open the bus front door.

The creature roared. The sound gave me chills.

Everyone started to rush out. Anitosh ran as soon as I opened the door, while I ran behind everyone. We went into the woods.

We looked behind us and saw the creature chasing us while groaning and roaring. We couldn't see the creature as much as we could hear its footsteps and groans.

We kept running into the woods. We were running on a very muddy soil.

"It's better to split up and run in different directions. At least half people will be saved." The man said breathlessly while running.

"No way. It's not a good idea. Let's run in a group so that even if it catches one of us, we can help each other in defending ourselves." Rishitha said.

We nodded, agreeing to Rishitha. We kept running into the woods sliding through the trees using our torches. We made thud sounds while running in the woods as we were running on wet soil and grass.

"What can that one creature do when there are eight of us? We should all stick together." Rahul said.

"We can't take the Red-eyed creature that easily," The man said in anger, looking at us.

We heard the creature coming closer to us. The sound of the creature groaning kept increasing and we started to run even faster with fear.

After some time of running, we couldn't hear the sounds of the creature anymore.

"Guys, I think the creature lost us," I said.

Everyone listened carefully.

"Yes!" Anitosh shouted

"Shhh" Rishitha whispered.

"Ha - ha, Look how fast we are. The creature couldn't even catch us. It isn't even close to us." Rahul said.

" You can't take a Red-eyed creature for granted. Who knows it might just be planning a sneak attack on us." The man groaned.

We were in the middle of the woods with trees all around us. The soil was muddy and the wind was getting colder. All that was helping us see were the moonlight and the torches. My heart was pounding. I could also hear everyone's heart pounding. We tried to breathe for some time. The trees were in different sizes, some thin, some thick, some tall, and some big, and most of the trees were tilted and curved.

It was the first time I'd been to this dark woods. Every small sound made me and my friends very alert and cautious.

"We can't waste any time right now. It's time to set up a trap to capture the Red-eyed creature." Rishitha said breathlessly

"Yes, But how do we trap it?" I asked

"All I could figure out was that it was afraid of the light. We just have to trap it till the morning. So that we can stay at peace till then." Rishitha said.

"Yes," I said.

Everyone else except the man nodded.

"It's not going to be that easy to trap the Red-eyed creature." The man groaned

"We have to try our best. That's the only option we have. We can't just give up" I said.

"Okay, what's the plan Rishitha? How do we trap it?" Anitosh asked.

"I don't know. We have to figure it out." Rishitha said.

"Do you think we should make weapons?" Rahul asked.

"We can't make weapons in such a short period. Also, creating weapons will create a lot of noise," Rishitha said.

"How about we just split up and run far away so that the Red-eyed creature will get confused?" The man said, staring at us.

"No, that's a terrible idea," Rishitha said.

Is the man trying to separate us? I thought. Why does he want us to split up?

"How about we trap it in the bus?" Anitosh asked.

"It will easily escape" Rishitha replied.

"Do you guys have any traps in your car?" Rahul asked, looking at the man.

"No, why would we carry traps in the car?" The man said with irritation.

"I have seen a few movies in which they capture animals. I might know a trick to trap the creature." I said.

"What is it?" Anitosh asked immediately.

Everyone looked for the answer.

"We can use the classic old trick of digging a hole in the ground, luring the creature into the hole, and trapping it," I said.

"Yes, we can do it," Rahul said with excitement

"Yes, we can also do it fast as there are 8 people here," I said.

"But, what about the equipment?" Rishitha asked.

"We can dig with our hands. It will be painful for sure but I think this is the only option left." I said.

"With our hands?" Supriya asked.

"The soil is a little muddy and wet due to the rain. I think it's an added advantage for us." I said.

"Let's get started. We can't afford to waste time now." Rahul said.

He started digging.

"Wait, what if the creature is near us? Shouldn't we just keep running?" The man asked.

"No, let's keep digging for now. If the creature comes back, we will run towards the

bus. Make sure you guys run towards the bus and not into the woods. We can get lost easily." I said.

I got down and started helping Rahul dig. We were moving our hands very fast.

Anitosh, Supriya, Nitish, and Rishitha joined us.

"I can't dig the soil. My jeans will get spoiled." The woman complained.

We kept digging. We began to take soil and throw it out very far. Just after a few minutes of digging, my hands started to hurt and I was getting tired. My stomach was growling. I heard Anitosh's stomach growling as well. We looked at each other and laughed. We were tired and in pain but we kept digging. I didn't know digging in wet soil would be so hard.

We dug out until we created a pit-like structure. We all got tired. The pit was around 4ft deep.

"Do you think this is enough?" Anitosh asked breathlessly

"Mostly," I said.

"The creature is only 3ft tall and this is not wide enough for the creature to run and jump," Rahul said.

"What if the creature just walks over this hole?" Supriya asked.

"I think we can keep someone on top of it when the creature falls in the hole so it does not escape", I said.

"What could it be?" Rishitha asked.

"Something heavy and wide enough to cover this hole", I said.

We started looking around. I kept my torch on the muddy ground and started looking around. All I could see were just mud, grass, and bugs crawling. The man and the wife just sat under a tree and kept talking while we were doing all the work. We didn't bother them.

I went a little too far from the group trying to find something to cover the pit and I went back near the pit we dug. Everyone was near the hole except for Anitosh.

"Where's Anitosh?" I shouted.

Everyone looked at me.

"Somewhere nearby," Rahul said while looking at the ground.

"Guys, I can't see Anitosh," I said.

Everyone looked at me.

"Really?" Rahul said.

"Anitosh!!" Rahul shouted.

We didn't hear back from him.

"Anitosh — Anitoshh!!" I shouted.

No reply. We were tense.

"We forgot to watch out for each other while trying to find an object." Rishitha said in a frightened voice.

Everyone kept shouting for Anitosh. The man and the wife came near us.

"What happened? Why are you guys shouting?" The man asked.

"Our friend Anitosh is missing," I said.

"Anitoshh!" Rishitha shouted.

"Oh no, what if—?" The man said.

We heard a scream. The voice was of Anitosh.

CHAPTER 18

We started running in the direction the voice came from. I was very tense and afraid.

Anitosh was one of my close friends in school. I couldn't lose him. I kept running as fast as I could. My legs felt like they were getting heated but I kept running. My friends were also running behind me. We ran towards the sound, trying to tackle the trees as fast as we could. All of our friends were covered in mud and we were tired but we had to find our friend.

"We should have always kept an eye on each other," Rahul said breathlessly.

"I feel dumb for not being observant enough. I was too focused on finding something." Rishitha said.

We kept running while the cold wind blew against our chest every time we took a step, making it very hard to run.

We saw a light beam a little ahead. We saw Anitosh.

He was holding a huge piece of wood,

"Guys, Look what I found. We can use this to cover the hole." Anitosh said, smiling.

I sighed. All my friends sighed. I was happy to see my friend.

"Why did you disappear into the woods? Never go anywhere alone, Anitosh." I said breathlessly.

Everyone was trying to breathe all the air possible. We were completely breathless.

"Yes Anitosh, you idiot. Never leave us like this." Rahul shouted breathlessly.

"What happened?" Anitosh asked.

"We thought you were lost so we ran when we heard you scream," I said.

"Sorry — sorry. I was too focused on finding something that I forgot about." Anitosh said while scratching the back of his head.

"Great, let's go back now," I said.

I was happy to see my friend again in good shape. We walked back to the hole we dug. The man and the wife didn't come with us. They were still near the hole we dug. We were using our flashlights for the way to be visible.

It was dark. I never thought I would be spending a night in the dark woods. It was around midnight. The cold winds dropped down the temperature. What we thought was easy was going to get harder if the cold would increase with time.

Rahul and Anitosh were both dragging the piece of wood that Anitosh found. It would be perfect to cover the hole.

" We should take some heavy rocks with us, to keep them on the wood. If you guys have any heavy rocks, pick them up." I said while walking.

Everyone nodded. I had no more energy to walk. Rishitha and Supriya were in front of me. I was in the middle and Anitosh, Rahul, and Nitish were walking behind me. I saw some rocks under the trees and on our way there. I picked them up as I was going.

We reached the place where we dug out the hole. The man and the woman were still under the tree, talking. They started to come near us when they saw us.

"So, did you find your friend?" The man asked.

I nodded and threw all the rocks near the hole.

We got the wood and placed it on the hole and saw that it perfectly covered the entire hole except for one edge. It was a rectangular piece of wood.

"That little open edge shouldn't matter. I don't think it can escape from there." I said.

"Yes, we have to keep the rocks on as soon as we keep the wood. If we delay, we could lose our lives." Rishitha said.

We got a little tense after hearing it.

I suddenly felt that someone was watching me and it got me chills all over my body. I looked behind, I used the phone torch and looked around. No one was there. I sighed

"What happened?" Anitosh asked.

"Nothing." I said.

I felt it again, the feeling of someone looking at me.

I then took my torch and looked up at the trees. I screamed. There it was the Red-eyed creature.

"It has set its eyes on me," I said.

"What?" Rahul asked.

"The creature," I said.

It was staring at me and grinning. All my friends saw the creature. They gasped. The man and the woman got up from under the tree and started running backward.

"Take a few steps back." I whispered. "Make sure you keep the wood and rocks ready to capture it once it falls in. Cover it with the wood and immediately keep the rocks on the edges."

My friends kept going back. Rahul, Nitish, and Anitosh were holding the wood.

The creature howled. The sound of the howl made everyone panic. Everyone was shivering. I kept taking steps backward making sure to not fall into the hole and looking into the Red-eyes of the creature.

The creature jumped down from the tree. I started running towards the hole. I passed the hole sideways and the creature jumped above the hole, the creature pushed me and got on top of me. I screamed at the top of my lungs while closing my eyes.

CHAPTER 19

I ran sideways from the hole and looked backward. The creature has jumped across the hole. The creature pushed me to the ground. The back of the head hit the ground. It was painful. The creature was on top of me. I couldn't bear the foul smell. I thought I was going to die.

All my friends looked at me and screamed out loud.

Rahul picked up the stones to throw at the creature. Rishitha immediately took out her torch and pointed it toward the eyes of the creature.

The torchlight made the creature take a few steps back and it fell into the hole we dug.

Nitish and Anitosh got the wooden plank and covered the hole. Supriya and Rahul put down the rocks on the plank.

I got up. My friends were really quick, I thought. We kept moving backward looking at the hole. There was no sign of the creature. It didn't move or try to get up.

"Thanks everyone," I said.

Everyone was still focused looking toward the hole. The wooden plank started shaking. The creature was trying to get out. We kept taking steps backward.

"Everyone! pick up the stones and rocks from the ground." I shouted.

The creature kept trying to come out, hitting the wooden plank harder and harder each time.

"We have to put more rocks on the plank or the creature will get out. Rahul shouted.

"Let me do it," I said.

I ran towards the hole carrying some rocks I found on the ground. The creature kept hitting the wooden plank. Every hit gave me chills. My legs were shivering when I went near the hole. I put down more rocks on the plank.

"Let me also help you," Rishitha said.

She walked towards the hole. The creature kept hitting its head and the wooden planks started to shake even more.

"Should we run now?" Rahul asked.

I saw through the small open edge of the hole. I saw the eyes of the creature very closely. I was terrified. I stepped backward. It was filled with anger, I thought. Rishitha also put some more rocks on the plank. She brought some very heavy rocks.

The creature was still hitting the plank but it didn't impact the plank as much as before. The creature stopped trying.

"Is this it? Did we capture the creature?" Rahul shouted.

"Maybe, not sure," Rishitha said.

I wanted to run as far as possible from the creature even if we trapped it. I couldn't open my mouth anymore. My entire body was trembling with fear.

"Let's go back to the bus now," I said with great difficulty

"Where are the adults?" Rahul asked.

We haven't seen them since a while.

"I— don't know. Let's just go now," Rishitha said.

There were no more sounds or signs of the creature trying to come out. We started going back towards the road from the woods. We used the torch lights of the phone. No one ever looked sideways with the torch due to fear. We just kept going back. We were getting the direction back to the road through the footsteps. We were trying to spot the footsteps which were made while running from the creature and following it back. We saw someone approaching us from far away.

"Someone is coming." Rahul said and bent down and took rocks.

I also started collecting rocks and pointed them toward the people who were coming.

It was the couple.

"What happened? Are you kids safe?" The man shouted.

We sighed looking at them.

"Yes, we are going back to the bus now." Rahul groaned.

"Is the creature trapped?" The man asked

"Yes," Rahul said. "Most probably".

"Let's go back and check," The man said, coming closer to us.

"Why?" I asked.

"We will be at risk going back to the road if the creature is still out. We need to confirm that we trapped it," The man said.

We didn't go that far from the hole. I thought it was better to check so that I could be at peace.

We went back to the hole and watched through the edge.

CHAPTER 20

We took a step forward and looked through the edge. All we could see was darkness.

The man put his torch into the hole. I was afraid to look but I could see the brown hair.

The creature was still there. It closed its eyes and was still in the hole. We cheered up. I jumped out of excitement even though my legs were in pain.

"Yes, we did it," Anitosh said.

"Shhh, let's just talk quietly," Rishitha whispered.

"Wooo, we did it," Rahul said.

"You kids trapped this creature, Wow!" The woman said.

"Yes, we did it," Supriya said.

"Okay, let's go back now," Rishitha whispered.

"But, what about our friends and teachers?" I asked.

I saw everyone's happiness turn into sadness when I asked that question. Maybe, I shouldn't have asked. I was happy to trap the animal but I still wanted to know what happened to them and how we were going to find them.

"All we can do is wait for the sunrise and figure it out in the daytime." Rishitha said " We will also get help in the daytime. It would be easier then. Let's keep moving now."

Everyone nodded.

We started moving back in the direction of our footprints, towards the road.

"Rishitha, what's the time now?" I asked.

"It's 2.32 AM," She said.

It was still very dark. The cool wind still blew across the woods. We couldn't stop anywhere for more than one minute as mosquitos would swarm us otherwise. We kept walking. I couldn't feel my legs anymore. All I knew was that I was walking with my friends. The couple was following behind us.

"Oh god, it's a long wait." Anitosh said with a sad tone.

"You shouldn't speak, you slept for a long time on the bus," Rahul said and laughed.

"No, I didn't." Anitosh said.

"Yes, you did," Nitish said and laughed.

"I was just meditating to be calmer," Anitosh said.

We all laughed.

"Meditating? What kind of meditation makes you groan while your eyes are closed?" Rahul asked while laughing.

"That's my style of meditation," Anitosh said "I wasn't even groaning, Rahul."

We kept laughing while walking to the road. The couple also were laughing when I looked back.

We could see the road. The long and silent road. We went on the road but we couldn't see the bus.

"Where is the bus?" Anitosh asked.

"We reached the road. The bus could be to the left or right of us," Rishitha said.

"I can't walk anymore," I said.

"Oh no, I can't walk anymore," Supriya said.

"After all the walking and running from the trip and in the woods, my legs can't move another step forward." Anitosh said.

"There is no other way but to go both directions and check," Rishitha said.

"Let's divide up. A few people go left and a few go right to find the bus. This way, we can find the bus faster." The man said.

"No, whatever happens, we stick together," Rishitha said.

The man smiled wickedly.

"Oh, darling! It would take a lot of time to find the bus if we stick together. It would be easier to find the bus if we divide and go separate ways and shout when any one of the groups finds the bus." The man said.

His wicked smile was very creepy. I didn't want to trust him.

"I agree with Rishitha. We should go together. First, let's go towards the left as I am sure we turned right when we were running before."

"Yes, let's go together towards the left," Rahul said.

The man sighed. We all started to walk to the left. We kept walking for around 20 minutes and there was no sign of the bus.

"I don't think the bus is towards the left. I think we should have gone towards the right." Anitosh said.

"Yes, we took the wrong turn," Rahul said.

"Uh kids, it would have been even so much better if you just listened to me. Look how far we have to walk now." The man said and groaned.

I was completely exhausted.

"I am sorry, I thought the bus was towards the left," I said.

"It's okay. Let's go towards the right now" Rishitha said.

"Can't we just sleep under this tree? Let's just sleep here." The man said.

"Sure, you guys can sleep but I heard that there will be snakes roaming in the woods tonight," Rahul said.

"Snakes!!! Now I don't want to hear any other dangerous stuff." Anitosh said.

The couple groaned. We started walking towards the right now. We didn't know how far the bus would be. I also remembered something. We didn't even close the doors of the bus. I just hope that there are no mosquitoes or any other animals on the bus.

We started to walk. We kept walking after another 20 minutes in the opposite direction.

"I can't walk anymore. I just can't." Anitosh said.

"Me too, I just want to lay down on this road," Rahul said.

I saw everyone was tired. Rishitha, Supriya, and Nitish were trying their best to walk but I could see that they were tired.

"It's not good for your health to sleep outside in this cold weather. Let me go alone and find the bus. Once I do. I will come back and shout. Till then you guys can rest here." I said.

"No, no way," Anitosh shouted immediately. "Let's just keep walking together."

"Yes, even if we are tired. We won't let you go alone." Rishitha said.

"Let's all go together, we should be able to find the bus very soon," Rahul said.

We walked for another 10 minutes on the cold windy night road. The wind made everyone cover their clothes tighter, sometimes the wind would make the trees shake heavily. That was the only other sound we could hear except for our footsteps and heartbeats. We looked down at each other to make sure we all were safe.

We saw it. We saw the bus in front of us. We ran towards the bus. I was in front of everyone. I ran towards the bus.

"Wait!" I shouted.

"What happened now?" Rahul asked.

"There might be some animals inside the bus. Let's hit the bus to check." I said.

Even in this cold wind & sleepiness, I didn't want to haste and make mistakes.

"Good idea," Rishitha said.

We all kept hitting the side of the bus. Nothing came out. We celebrated. The couple tried to start their car but their car didn't start. They came out of their car and ran into the bus.

All of us entered the bus. It was peaceful as ever. I was also a little shocked that no animals entered the bus for shelter.

I saw the couple immediately dozing off to sleep. There were still mosquitoes but not a lot of them. I closed the door but the broken window was still open. We didn't care.

Everyone got in their seats and sighed with relief.

"Man, I wasn't able to feel the pain in my legs before. But now they are burning." Nitish said.

"Anitosh, It's time for you to start meditating," Rahul said.

We laughed.

"Stop it," Anitosh said.

Slowly everyone dozed off to sleep.

I woke up with someone shaking my shoulders. I opened my eyes.

CHAPTER 21

"Hey, wake up. Wake up, Darsh, wake up. It's about to be morning." Anitosh said while shaking my shoulders.

I woke up and all my friends and the couple were already awake. "What's the time now?" I asked

"5:21 AM," Rishitha said.

"10 more minutes to sunrise," Anitosh exclaimed.

I looked outside. It was still as dark as midnight. The moonlight became dimmer than the night.

"Why is it still so dark outside? Shouldn't we at least see a little light by now?" Rahul asked

"Maybe because we are in the woods," Rishitha said.

The sun rises every day before 5:40 in our town.

"I am happy, we just have to wait for 10 more minutes or 20 minutes maximum," Anitosh said.

I took out my water bottle and drank water from that. We were just looking outside and the time kept passing.

"At what time do you think other travelers will come on this road?" I asked, looking at the man.

"I don't know but I think people should start traveling from 6.30 AM. I guess," The man said.

"Our parents must be very worried. They would rush to the police as soon as the morning hits." Anitosh said.

"Yes," Rahul said.

"I hope they find us fast," Supriya said.

"Will they even believe our story? It all seems so crazy," Anitosh said.

"I still can't understand anything. Let's hope they come and find us so that we can go in search of our friends" I said.

I started to get more worried. Why did the sun still not rise? Why is it so late on the day we need it the most?

It's been more than 10 minutes and it still was as dark as a night.

"Why isn't there any sunlight by now?" Anitosh asked.

"Maybe the sun is still meditating like you," Rahul laughed. It was a very forced laugh

"I don't know. It might take time to rise due to the hills on our right." Rishitha said.

We kept looking for the sunrise. It's been more than 20 minutes now.

"What's the time now?" I asked.

"It's 5:56 AM," Rishitha said.

"Woo, the sun should have been up by now," Anitosh said in worry.

"Yes, it should be up by now," Supriya said.

"Why isn't the sun up?" Rahul groaned.

"Let's wait for a few more minutes," Rishitha said.

We waited for 10 more minutes and it was still as dark as midnight.

"Let's get off the bus, we might see the sunlight and the sunrise," The man suggested.

We got down on the bus. It was as clear as the night, The moonlight was dim, yet we

couldn't see the sun. We looked around the edges of the sky but not even a ray of sunlight was to be seen. In the horrifying darkness and chilly winds,

We realized that the sunrise is missing.

CHAPTER 22

We looked around the edges of the sky but not even a ray of sunlight was seen. In the horrifying darkness and chilly winds,

We realized that the sunlight was missing.

It was dark like midnight just started. The wind was still very cool.

"How could this happen? How come the sun isn't up yet?" Anitosh stammered.

I was speechless.

"Does the creature have the power to stop even the sun from rising?" Anitosh asked with a worried tone.

It took me a few minutes to settle in and understand the situation. So did everyone. We were just staring.

"Guys, what's happening? Anitosh shouted.

"I — don't — know," I said looking at him

"How could the sun possibly disappear?" Rahul asked.

"Does the creature have the power to stop the sun?" Supriya asked

The man looked at her. The man was still in shock. I tapped on him.

"Does the creature have this power?" I asked the man.

"No— no. This is impossible," The man stammered.

"We are in the middle of nowhere and there is not even a ray of sun. I think this is our end," Anitosh cried out.

"How is this even possible?" Rishitha asked.

"Am I still dreaming?" Nitish asked while in shock.

I started to smell the foul smell again.

"Can you guys also smell it?" Anitosh asked.

We looked at each other.

We heard someone running from the woods. We started to take steps backward. The foul smell kept increasing.

The creature came in front of us from the woods with its wicked smile looking at us

We all screamed. We didn't even have time to think.

"Run!" I shouted.

We looked back to see more creatures. We looked towards the left and there were more creatures and more towards the right. There were hundreds of creatures surrounding us. We were in the middle of the road and we kept turning our flashlights and saw a lot of creatures surrounding us. Everywhere we looked we saw the creatures. Their wicked smile, their bright red eyes, and the drops of saliva and blood from their mouth.

They circled us, trapping us.

"Oh — this would explain how your teachers and friends disappeared," The man said.

CHAPTER 23

The creatures were getting close to us.

"What do we do now?" Rahul cried out.

I saw a very little opening in between the creatures, in the woods. I pointed my torch there.

"Let's run towards that opening," I shouted

"Hold up your torches and start running," Rishitha said.

We all pointed our torches in a direction and started running into the woods. We all kept screaming while running. We were running with no plan whatsoever.

The couple was fast, they kept running and they were at the front. Rahul, Nitish, and Anitosh were running fast as well. I couldn't run as fast as them. I was running beside Rishitha and Supriya.

The creature started running towards us, howling. The sounds of the howl gave me chills all down my spine. Each howl sounded like a death alarm ringing.

I heard someone shouting and falling to the ground. I looked back and it was Supriya. A creature pushed her. I immediately stopped and used the torch on the creature's eyes, ran towards it, and kicked it with my feet. I lifted Supriya and we started running again. There were a lot of creatures behind us. We both were very close to the creatures. We both could hear the grinning of the creatures.

We both couldn't see any of our friends in front. We all got separated. I saw that Supriya was a little hurt. She wasn't able to run as fast as before.

"Supriya, I am going to distract the creatures towards the right. Please make sure you keep going straight and find our friends," I shouted while running.

"No, don't," She shouted while she was struggling to run.

"We will meet very soon, I promise," I shouted.

I looked back, threw a rock at the creatures, and started running toward the right. A lot of creatures turned toward me. Almost all of the creatures in the front started following me. I was happy that now Supriya can join the group.

I kept running as fast as possible in the woods, I had a very close call with hitting a tree in the woods. The mud was still very wet making it hard to run.

I ended up in front of a cave and huge rocks. There was nowhere else to go. Behind me were the creatures. I had to go into the cave, I thought. I hoped that there would be an exit to this cave and started running.

As I was running into the cave, I started to hear the sounds of someone crying. The sounds of the crying kept echoing throughout the entire cave. The sound was like a baby crying. I kept running into the cave. The closer I went into the cave, the sound of the crying kept increasing. I looked back with my torch to see if the creatures were still following me. I saw the creatures still coming after me. My leg hit a very hard rock-like substance and I toppled over.

I pointed my torch back and looked back again to see a kid sitting in the middle of the cave.

The kid had red eyes just like the creatures. He was half my height. He had 3 fingers on his hands and only 2 toes and he was half naked.

He looked at me and even cried more. I was shocked and confused. The creatures were getting very close. I went to the kid, helped him get up, took his hand, and started running. We kept running and saw the cave's dead end in front of me.

My biggest nightmare came true. The dead end of the cave. I went forward to somehow tackle the creatures to my best and save the kid. The creatures slowly stepped forward grinning and they pushed me and fell on top of me.

CHAPTER 24

The creatures were on top of me. Liquid and blood dripped down from their mouth. I heard the sounds of digital buttons. I turned my head to see that the kid was pressing some button on a weird device he had.

I looked back and saw that all the creatures had disappeared, just vanished. I was surprised.

The kid started crying even more. The sounds of his cries echoed through the entire cave. I thought this kid had to be the reason for the creatures to disappear. I went up to him.

"Hey, let's get out of this cave," I said and smiled.

I didn't want to ask him questions and bother him. He kept crying. We both started to walk toward the entrance of the cave. It was still very dark. My mobile's battery is just 2% now. I hope that the torch at least stays on till I meet my friends. I hope they escaped safely from the creatures.

The kid stopped crying after some time. I looked at him. He had no hair and his head and was larger than any human I saw.

We both reached the entrance of the cave. I heard my friends and the couple coming a little far from the cave.

"Anitosh!" I shouted.

They all started running towards me.

"The creatures disappeared," Anitosh shouted while running.

"Yess! We don't know how but they did," Rahul shouted.

"Thank god you are safe Darsh, thank you," Supriya shouted while running.

They came near me.

"Who is the kid? And why are his eyes like the red-eyed creature?" Rahul asked, looking at the kid weirdly and stepping backward.

"I don't know. I think he is the reason for the vanishing of all the creatures." I said.

"How?" Rishitha asked.

"He used a device of his and the creatures vanished," I said.

"Is he an alien?" Anitosh stammered.

"I think so," I said.

Everyone gasped and stepped backward. The kid got a little stressed looking at them.

"I think he is a good alien, he saved us all right?" I said.

"Where and how did you find him?" The man asked suspiciously.

"In the cave, while I was running," I said. I was still holding his hand. He stopped crying but still had tears in his eyes.

"Maybe he is the reason all those creatures appeared in the first place," Rahul shouted in an angry voice.

"Can he speak?" Anitosh asked.

"Yes," The kid said in the sweetest voice I ever heard. It was a very smooth, sweet, and soothing voice. The voice was very pleasant to hear.

I then realized that he could speak English. I was surprised. I looked at everyone and they were surprised and were in awe at the kid's voice.

"Who are you?

"How did you get in here?"

"What happened to your parents?"

"How do you know English?"

"Are you behind our missing friends and teachers too?" We bombarded him with questions. I was curious and confused.

The kid looked at me.

"I am lost," The kid cried out.

"How? What happened?" Rishitha asked suspiciously

"I am not from this planet. My Mother and Father visited this planet every once in a while for their research. When they were leaving my planet, I snuck into their machine. They didn't know that I was there and I came here. I snuck out of the machine to explore and they both went home with the machine. Now I am lost here," The kid said with a sad voice.

"Are you the reason for all the things that happened yesterday night?" I asked.

He nodded.

We all were in shock.

"Why did you do all that? Why did you torture us all?" Rahul groaned and asked.

"It was fun," The kid said and laughed.

"Torturing us seemed funny to you?" Rahul asked and started coming toward him with an angry face.

He raised his hand to beat him up. I tried to stop him.

The kid pressed a few more buttons in his device and Rahul started to float in the air.

"Get me down, get me down!" He shouted while shaking his hands and legs in the air.

The kid giggled.

"Get him down please, I won't let him beat you," I assured the kid.

He pressed a few more buttons and he put Rahul down.

The kid started crying again. We all were very angry with him but also understood that he was lost on another planet and he had no one else.

"I have nowhere to go, my parents left me. I can't go back to my planet." The kid cried out.

"Don't worry kid, we are with you," I said.

"But you guys will never accept me for who I am. Mom used to say a lot of things about the Earth. She says humans are not trustworthy." The kid said.

"You are one of us and we won't leave your side until you find your parents, I promise." I said and patted his back. He looked at me and cried even more. I didn't know what to do. He hugged me.

Everyone had a warm smile on their faces. I felt very emotional when he hugged me.

"What's your name?" I asked him.

"Can you also please bring back the sun and our friends?" Rishitha asked.

"Sure," The kid said.

He pressed a few buttons on his device. That was a transparent mobile-like strutted device that had blue light symbols on them.

A hemispherical layer-like hologram started to tear out from the ground. While it was tearing out, we could see the rays of the sunlight appear. We all jumped out of joy.

We could see the sun again. The sunlight was falling on us. It felt warm again and the fresh air hit us. We felt fresh again taking huge and happy breaths. It was a feeling of pure joy.

"Can you also bring back our teachers and friends?" I asked.

He pressed a few more buttons and then we heard the sounds of the crashing trees and the sound of the bus. The bus was coming into the woods near us. It came right in front of us and stopped. We all were surprised to see that.

"How did you even do that?" Anitosh asked.

The trunk of the bus opened and we saw all our friends and teachers there. I sighed. I never knew so many people could fit in a bus trunk.

"We thought of everything but didn't even check the bus trunk!" Supriya said and laughed.

"Yes, we are dumber than we thought," I said.

The kid pressed a few more buttons and a transparent helmet-like structure got off our teacher's and friends' heads one by one. We helped them get out of the bus trunk.

Everyone got off the bus but didn't fully understand what exactly was happening. They kept looking all around.

"What even happened, where are we at?" A student asked while looking around.

"It's a very long story," Rishitha said

"And we don't have the energy to explain it all now," Anitosh said.

A few students stared at the kid and were grossed out.

"Ew, who is that?" A student said.

"Why does he look so weird?" Another student asked.

The kid held onto my hands tightly.

"He is our new friend from a different world," I said while smiling.

The teachers and students were in shock.

"What?" A student shouted.

CHAPTER 25

The kid hid behind me when he heard the shouting and was ready to press buttons on his device.

"Yes, he got separated from his parents when they came here to explore. And we need to keep him safe till his parents come back." Rishitha said.

"We are in the woods. We got attacked by some creatures and all of you guys went unconscious. This kid saved us all," I said.

"Really? We all went unconscious? Just by looking at a creature?" A student asked suspiciously.

"Yes, don't you guys remember anything?" Rahul asked and giggled.

"Okay, now how do we get out of here, students?" The principal asked.

The kid pressed a few more buttons and the bus's flat tire returned to normal.

"Now it's easy to get home," I said.

"Let's go quickly, your parents must be very worried about you guys. Hop onto the bus immediately. We can discuss more on the bus." The principal said in a very loud voice.

"Can you please also drop us near our car?" The man asked the principal.

"Who are you guys?" The principal asked.

"As the kids said, it's a very long story," The man said.

Principal gasped.

"Okay whatever, Get on the bus immediately," the Principal said.

We all got on the bus one by one. Me, Anitosh, Supriya, Rahul, Nitish, Rishitha, and the Kid were all seated at the back of the bus. The bus started up and it reached the road where the couple found their car.

The kid pressed a few more buttons and the car started even before the couple got off the bus.

"Thank you," They shouted and got in the car. We waved our hands and the bus started.

"He looks different, don't you think villagers are going to beat him when they see him?" Anitosh asked.

I wondered that too. How can we manage that?

The kid pressed a few more buttons and his look changed to exactly like a human. We were surprised by it.

"Problem solved," I said.

"What's your name?" I asked, looking at the kid.

"My name is 48E349D," He said.

"That's not what we call each other on Earth", Rahul said.

"Your name till you stay with us on Earth is — is — Taj," I said looking at him.

He smiled.

The principal called Rishitha in the front, where he was seated and asked her to explain everything that had happened. She explained everything in detail to the Principal and asked him if he could let Taj stay in the town till his parents showed up. The principal first disagreed but after some time of contemplating, he agreed.

We were almost near the village. We saw police vehicles all over. It was a mess entering the village. All our parents were worried to death. We got off and they all hugged their kids and kissed them. My mom came running toward me and saw that I was in good shape. I was hurt a little here and there but it wasn't a big deal. She teared up seeing me back.

"Mom, this is Taj. He is lost. Can he stay with us till his parents show up?" I asked Mom.

"Sure," She said.

I guess she was very happy seeing me back that she let someone else stay in my house because that would never have happened otherwise.

I waved at all my friends while going back.

"See you all at school!" I shouted.

"Yes, you too," Rahul shouted.

"You too, Taj," Anitosh shouted.

"Take rest, all of you," Rishitha shouted.

"Thanks for everything," Supriya shouted.

"Make sure you bring your device to school Taj," Nitish shouted.

And we all waved our hands and headed home.

CHAPTER 26

After a few days —

It was a bright and sunny day. I woke up, and packed my school bag and lunch. Taj and I started school. It felt very good to be out in the sunlight and feel the rays of the sun on our bodies.

We both reached school and I saw the bus driver.

"Taj, I will be back in a second. Can you go to the class?" I asked.

He nodded.

I started walking toward the bus driver. I completely forgot about Raghav. He gave me a watch of his, which I forgot to return. When I think of it, I never saw Raghav on the bus while coming back or even after going home.

I went up to the bus driver. He was cleaning the bus exteriors. I called him and showed him the watch.

"Here is the watch Raghav gave me on the bus. Sorry, it's broken." I said to the driver.

"Who is Raghav?" He asked, wondering

"Your son, uncle," I said.

"Ha, good joke kid. My son is a working professional who is working in a city now," He said.

I was confused and then I thought it was one of the tricks by Taj.

"Okay uncle, Thanks," I said and went to class.

Taj and all of my friends were seated at the back benches. I walked towards Taj and sat beside him.

"So, what's your age, Taj?" Anitosh asked. I forgot to ask this question.

"321 Qantas," Taj said.

"What?" I asked. Everyone was surprised.

"Yes, we measure age differently on our planet," Taj said.

"Do you know how much that is on Earth?" I asked.

"Umm, 2 years," He said.

We were in shock now. Taj was just a 2-year-old kid, I wondered. He was very smart for a 2-year-old.

"What can your device do?" Rahul asked.

The teacher stepped into the class as Rahul asked the question.

"I will explain it later," Taj whispered.

He kept looking out the window at the sky all the time. He must be missing his parents and friends a lot.

"So, how did you create Raghav?" I whispered in class.

"Raghav?" He wondered as if he never knew who it was.

"Yes, the one who sat beside me at the start of the field trip," I whispered

"I don't know about that," Taj whispered.

All of a sudden, the weather started changing, The clouds covered the entire sun. It became completely dark outside. Thunderstorms started. The sound of the thunderstorm gave every student and teacher a chill. Everyone started looking outside.

Taj looked at me and smiled. I winked.

About the Author

Shaik Yaseen Ahmad is a young passionate author, who likes to explore different art forms like photography, writing, music production, editing, and many more. He believes in always trying new things and seeking growth and learning in everything he does.

At the age of 11, he created his first short film, sparking a lifelong passion and curiosity for creative expression. He participated in many competitions, made YouTube videos, gave presentations, started a business, learned marketing, and founded a college club to gain new experiences. He learns everything through YouTube videos, podcasts, movies and books

He has high ambitions and experiences the constant ups and downs of life, continually enhancing his understanding.

www.ingramcontent.com/pod-product-compliance
Lightning Source LLC
Chambersburg PA
CBHW031752150726
47989CB00006B/2688